Previously published as *HaMelech Amar* by Kinneret Publishing House, Ltd., in Israel in 2016. Translated from Hebrew by Annette Appel. First published in English by Amazon Crossing Kids in collaboration with Amazon Crossing in 2023.

Published by Amazon Crossing Kids, New York, in collaboration with Amazon Crossing

www.apub.com

Amazon, Amazon Crossing, and all related logos are trademarks of Amazon.com, Inc., or its affiliates.

ISBN-13: 9781662514289 (hardcover)
ISBN-13: 9781662514296 (eBook)

The illustrations were rendered in pencil, mono prints, and digital media.

Book design by AndWorld Design
Printed in China

First Edition
10 9 8 7 6 5 4 3 2 1

SIMON Says GOOD NIGHT

Written and illustrated by Orit Bergman
Translated by Annette Appel

amazon crossing kids

Daddy says: Brush your teeth.

Daddy says: Clean your ears.

Daddy says: Wash your feet.

Daddy says:
HANDS UP.

Daddy says:
HANDS DOWN.

Now, cover up,
close your eyes,
and go to sleep.

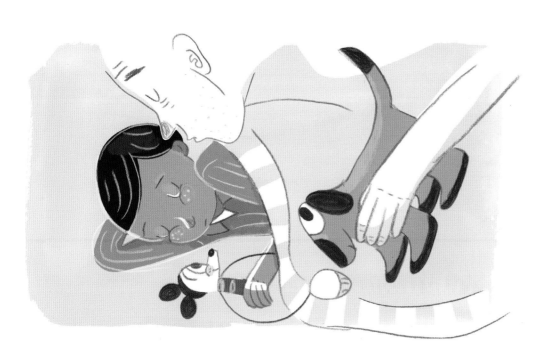

Good night, buddy.

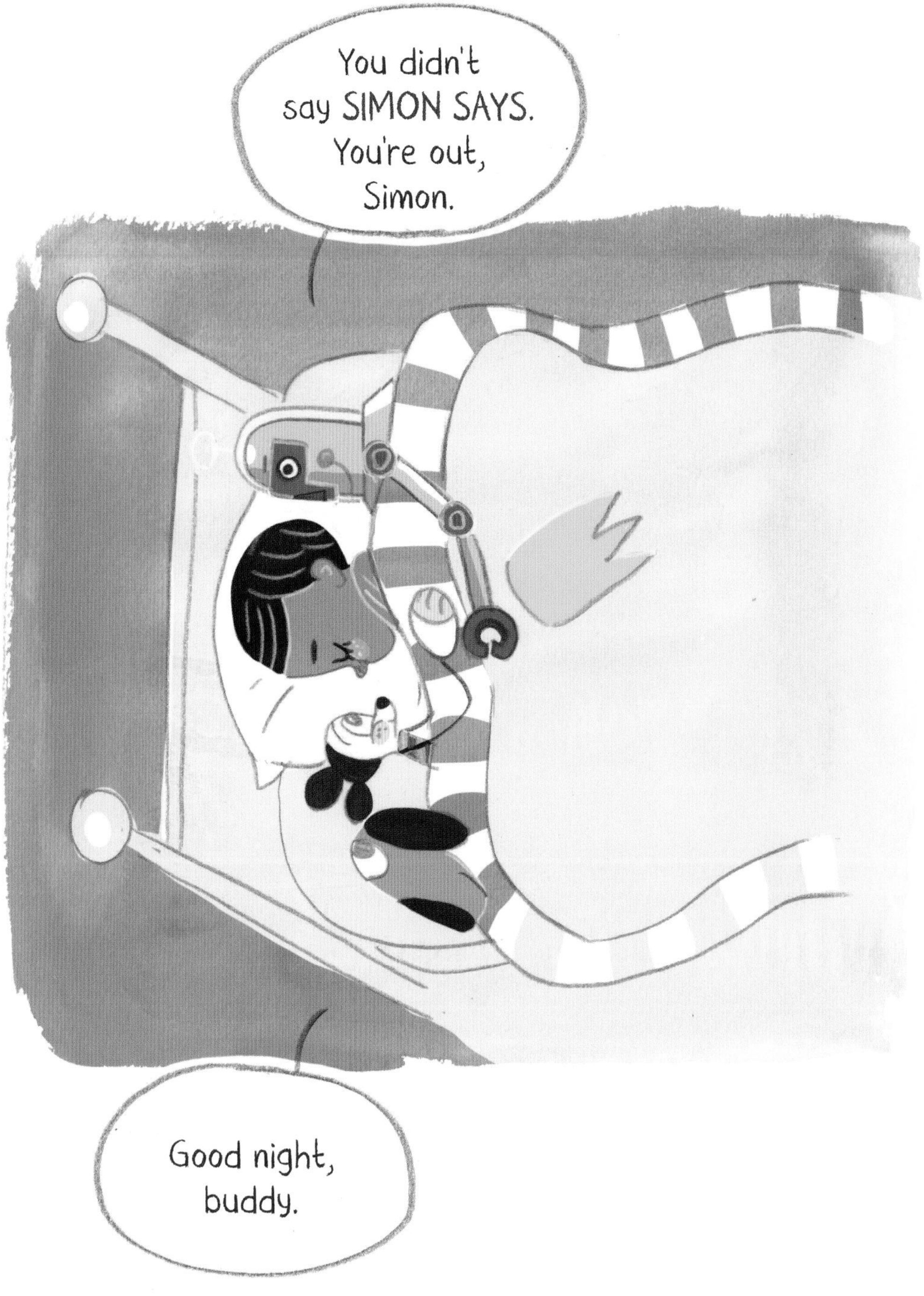
You didn't say SIMON SAYS. You're out, Simon.
Good night, buddy.